Just BREATHE
A Journey Through Grief

Written by
Wendy Archard

Illustrated by
Michelle Angela

Just Breathe: A Journey Through Grief
Copyright © 2023 by Wendy Archard

All rights reserved. No part of this publication may be reproduced, distributed, or transmitted in any form or by any means, including photocopying, recording, or other electronic or mechanical methods, without the prior written permission of the author, except in the case of brief quotations embodied in critical reviews and certain other non-commercial uses permitted by copyright law.

Tellwell Talent
www.tellwell.ca

ISBN
978-0-2288-8729-4 (Hardcover)
978-0-2288-8730-0 (Paperback)
978-0-2288-8728-7 (eBook)

Dedicated to my children
Jaden, Journey and Lily.

This book was inspired by the memory of
my daughter Journey, who passed away in 2018
when she was fifteen years old.
She was an amazing artist and a beautiful soul.
We love you and miss you forever.

Sometimes
it's hard to get through the day...

ever since
you passed away.

Sometimes I'm **angry** at not having you around.

Sometimes I cry out loud, and sometimes I make no sound.

I try to remember
what you told me to do
whenever I feel this way.

"Close your eyes,
take a deep breath in...

and when
you breathe out...
blow
the sadness
away".

Take another breath in and hold it in place.

I close my eyes
and **remember**
your beautiful face.

As I breathe out again, I smile, and I start to feel better...

thinking of all the good times we shared together.

It's OK to be sad and miss you, but I shouldn't stay **sad** for too long.

Although
I can't see you anymore
and we are apart...

I know you're
always with me
in a special place
in my heart.

I might feel **bad** again but I'll try my best to be OK.

Just breathe and repeat and...

CPSIA information can be obtained
at www.ICGtesting.com
Printed in the USA
JSHW070050200723
45061JS00008B/65

9 780228 887300